MW01268778

KAMDENGE
and
The Arrogant King

This is a Ugandan story about a homeless orphan and his pursuit to marry the most eligible Princess in the Kingdom. It is based on an adaptation of an ancient Lango folklore tale.

Author:
F M Abelkec-Lukonyomoi

DEDICATION

This book is dedicated to my grandchildren and all my loved ones born and growing up into the diaspora, who would have missed out on the privilege of listening to traditional oral storytelling "around the fire place" or under the mango trees.

TABLE OF CONTENTS

FORWARD

The 'Kamdenge and the Arrogant King' story originates from Northern Uganda and is a Lango folklore tale that I heard when I was a child. The story told was about Kamdenge and his friends, and how they met his challenge to marry the daughter of an arrogant king. In the original story, there was no mention of Kamdenge's parents or his heritage. This is why, in this story I have created a mother, who gave birth to him.

Folklore stories such as 'Kamdenge and the Arrogant King' is one of the traditional ways of imparting cultural knowledge and wisdom down through the generations. The story is intended to be educational, informative, as well as entertaining.

Story telling is good for educating school children from an early age, as well as for informing the general community and public to know and 'learn about past events, both good and bad. Furthermore, it is hugely important in helping us to understand the world, others and ourselves. "I have often thought how stories can help promote good mental health; they are a safe way of exploring difficult subjects, developing empathy and experiencing different times, places, and cultures. I really do believe that stories are for people of all ages!" (Pat Wilson 2020).

In this tale, 'Kamdenge and the Arrogant King' touches on the danger of autocratic rule, dictatorship and the power of war, and the distress it causes when people are forced to seek refuge and asylum in other countries. This, in turn causes immigration problems.

The story of 'Kamdenge and the Arrogant King' can be adapted to a play and could be performed in prisons and detention centres, where prisoners or the detainees would be able to identify with characters and the emerging story; giving them some hope, despite their painful experiences. For artists, engaging in 'Kamdenge and the Arrogant King' is also beneficial to them as it enables them to release any suppresed emotions through expressive art, as well as developing the skills to actualise their own self-worth.

PROLOGUE

The beginning of this story is based on an actual event that happened to a young woman, during civil unrest in Northern Uganda. There was an attack that the military had plotted to carry out on the members of our Church, which my family had built at Otwe, in Amuru, Uganda.

They wanted to destroy the infrastructure and development we had brought to Otwe. The Church building housed a school during the week and was fundamental to the community. The military's intention was to burn down the Church in its entirety, which they eventually did. On the same day as the Church was destroyed, they burnt down every single building in our homestead, Lubanga-Oyabo, including a clinic and various municipal buildings, granaries, and storages. Some of those buildings were used as wards for sick people, and others as residences for our family.

In the village there was a Health centre called, 'The Abundant Life Clinic.' Here, we served and met the health needs of the community from Otwe, and beyond; it also functioned as a maternity centre where women came from all over to give birth.

In collaboration with the Catholic Mission Health Centre at Amuru, we also ran a children's clinic where immunisation was carried out for the citizens of Otwe and the wider community. This clinic also catered for the health service needs of many of the armed forces, who could walk into the clinic without an appointment, to seek medical attention for war-field casualties and various ailments ranging from malaria, to sexually transmitted diseases.

One day, the military entered our home with the intention of removing or displacing all the males in my family. They had come to arrest my husband. On their arrival, the soldiers captured our first-born son, Richard, mistaking him for his father.

They tied my son, who was a young adult at the time, in their notorious 'Three Piece Style', a form of restraint whereby both hands of their victim were tied behind their back, with the arms forcefully pulled closely together and tied in three different places: at the wrists, the elbows and the upper arms. The arms were pulled so hard and tightly, that the chest was stretched extensively; they also interrogated the victim at the same time.

As chance would have it, their informer alerted them that they had got the wrong man, highlighting that they had captured the son instead; not the man they had come for. They then questioned our son again and asked why he was running when they arrived in the compound. Richard told them that he had been running to the market on some family errands. As soon as they relaxed their grip on him, he escaped and disappeared. I never saw my son again.

The soldiers then surrounded one of our houses, the very one in which my husband was hiding. It seemed that their informer had given them a good map of our homestead and its many buildings. Some of them had entered the exact room in which he was hiding, but they could not see him. He even coughed loudly from inside that little room, and one of the soldiers reported this to the commander, who became tongue-tied. Although the people being interrogated outside the house had clearly heard the cough, surprisingly, the commander did not give any orders. He could have commanded the soldiers to throw a hand grenade into the building and it was a miracle that he did not.

This incident then opened the door for multi-armed military groups to intermittently attack and raid our Lubanga Oyabo home; forcing the occupants, young and old alike, to keep running and hiding in bushes for many days and nights on end, over several months.

The Church became a target and it was repeatedly threatened with being burnt down because of its teachings, which resulted in female members rejecting the sexual advances of the soldiers.

Towards the end of 1987, while a group of women were returning from a market one evening, some armed military men singled out a prominent member of our Church, pulled her into the grass, and raped her.

The victim reported to us that the man who had raped her, already had fresh blood stains on his hands when he forced her into the grass. She was not sure if it was blood from killing someone. She was overwhelmed with fear that she may be pregnant or may have contracted sexually transmitted disease (STD) from this incident. This deeply terrifying ordeal traumatised her severely, especially since she was engaged to be married.

Around the same time, the Government ordered the residents of Amuru and the bordering village of Anaka, as well as many other parts of Northern Uganda, to immediately leave their homes and relocate to designated camps. Many Northern Ugandan people who were able, fled the country altogether, seeking refuge in foreign lands. Other people, who could not leave the country, desperately ran from one place to another to seek safety.

In addition to being uprooted, the young woman who had been sexually abused, carried the extra-heavy burden of the deep shame and severe guilt that the assault afflicted her. She was psychologically traumatised and plagued with embarrassment, as she was already engaged to be married. Unable to settle, like her fellow Ugandans, she ran from place to place; hiding from the community to cover up her guilt and shame.

****

This true story has been incorporated into the adaptation of Kamdenge's tale. The intention is to highlight the perils of military insurgency on citizens of a land, and its impact on both the young and old alike; where women and children usually, though unarmed defenseless citizens, suffer the most. This is one of many injustices and pains that add to the plight of refugees and asylum seekers, who look for a safe haven to rest from the weariness of their traumatic experiences.

It seemed befitting to include the story of Kamdenge's mother in here, portraying that the existence of the pregnancy had resulted from the rape of the young woman, during the insurgency on the country at the time. Being an unmarried mother was frowned upon in the community at the time. But carrying a child of a rapist carried an even greater stigma.

CULTURE AND CONTEXT

This story is adapted from the original ancient Lango folklore

Although this educational story was originally told in the local language, it has been translated into English, for the purpose of this project. Some of the characters in it are represented by animals and birds of multicultural backgrounds (such as of an interracial and intertribal marriages).

There is traditional singing, drumming and dancing in the story, alongside dialogue. Different languages are used in the tale, especially in the dirge singing. There are also some local Lango and Acoli dialects, derived from the original version.

LANGUAGE:

Translations of some of the local names, words and phrases.

Nicknames:

Awange-acel - one who has only one eye

Akome-ikoyo - One who is always freezing cold

Ayie-lyet / Ayie-odeng / Aie-lyet - One who is always hungry

Abade-bor – One who has long arm

Animals, nature, and beverages:

'Iwalu' - Crested Crane

'Amuka' - Rhino / rhinoceros

'Lyec' - Elephant

'Lyeci' – Elephants

'Dolo' - colobus monkey, its furry-skin is used as a dance costumes.

'Til' - Antelope: commonly known in Uganda as the 'Uganda cob', which appears on the Uganda Court of Arms. The hide, or skin of Til is treated or softened, and used as a dance costume. Many people in the countryside also use the dried hide of Til as a mat to sit or sleep on.

'Opobo' / 'pobo' - A kind of tree, which serves different purposes. Its seeded fruits are small, light green, and slightly sweet. Birds and children like to eat this, when they are about in the bush or grassland where the trees grow. Their tender branches are used as reeds for building material. The inner lining of **Opobo** is crushed and mixed with water to make leathery local hair shampoo. In the fifties and sixties, or even later, the tender branches of **pobo / opobo** were also used as whips for disciplining unruly children. The barks of fresh tender branches are used as ropes in building. The inner lining of the bark of the tender branches, or **opobo / pobo** reeds are used in weaving. The mature straight and longer **opobo** branches are cut and used as poles for axes and handheld hoes. The good mature main **pobo** trees trunks are used as poles for building works too. Then all parts of the dried **Opobo / Pobo** tree are excellent for firewood.

'**Lira-Lira**' / '**Arege**' is a very strong, distilled alcoholic drink that may be diluted and processed into the National '**Uganda Warege**'. It is named Lira-Lira because of its local origin, mainly by the Langi people of Lango, whose main town was called 'Lira'. This trade then became a main commercial strong alcoholic beverage, among many slum dwellers in Kampala, and elsewhere. The product was then supplied to the East African distilleries Ltd factory at Luzira, Port bell, by Lake Victoria, where it is processed into the 'National Uganda Warege'.

Phrases and sayings:

'**Mwoc**' – specific, but significant praise names (e.g. "**Chua**-yeeeee!" In this case, it's praising the clan "Chua"

'**mwoco mwoc**' uttering specific but significant praise names (e.g. "I am the daughter of the most prominent Chief, from the land of Chua, the land blessed with green pasture, my people are fearless, they are warriors. Do not mess with me or else you mess with fire!").

'**Ijira**' / '**Kijira**' A high pitched sound that women make from the back of their tongues and throats. This is a form of expressing extreme joyous happiness over a victorious occurrence, or a joyous complimenting of a singing and dance excitement. In Acoli (Acholi) culture, 'Kijira' may also be sounded as an encouragement to strengthen the men during a war dance, or as a sign of support for that course.

'Agana lam; twara ineno I wangi' (Lango dialect), this is one way to describe an overly crowded event venue, with the number of people over-filling the venue beyond description).

'Ojuk-kwe', is usually a name for an insistent or persistent person who does not listen to any instructions or warnings when being corrected, or someone who does not listen to anyone.

'Aboka lam; twara ineno ki wangi' (Acholi dialect), this is one way to describe an overly crowded event venue, with the number of people over-filling the venue beyond description).

'Langwidi matar rabo ki cen'! (Acholi dialect) this is one way to describe an overly crowded event venue, with the number of people filling the venue beyond capacity.

LANGO VERSUS ACOLI (ACHOLI) DIALECT

In this story, some words or names are used interchangeably between Acoli (Acholi) and Lango dialects. It helps, and it is right to know that there are two Northern Ugandan tribes, the Lango and the Acoli (Acholi) who both speak a similar language, generally known as, 'Lwo' (Luwo) as the Lango writes it, or 'Luo', which is a universal spelling across East Africa. There are very small differences in some words or names between these two languages. For instance, where Lango would say, 'Abade-bor' (one with long arm) the Acoli would say, 'Labade-bor'. Lango would say, 'Ayie-Lyet' or 'Ayie-odeng' (one who is ever hungry), but the Achoni would say, 'Layie odeng', 'Laie odeng 'or 'Laie lyet'. When Lango says, 'Akome-ikoyo' (one is always freezing cold), the Acoli would say, 'Lakome-kikoyo'. This is the same for, 'Awange-acel' (One who has only one eye) and, 'Lawange-acel'.

MUSIC AND DANCE

'**Larakarak**a', which is pronounced as, '**La-ra-ka-ra-ka**', is an Acholi courtship dance (e.g. https://www.youtube.com/watch?v=3stPR_Rlg8c).

'**Otole** 'is an Acoli war-dance (e.g. https://www.youtube.com/watch?v=sNmNFGvBBPE).

'**Acut**' is an Acholi all-female prayer dance (e.g. https://www.youtube.com/watch?v=RFC4xcGrjJc).

'**ciliki**' is the fork part of the music instrument called "Kilimba" / "Thumb Piano" – percussion instrument musical instrument. **Cilik**i is arranged like an elongated comb, made from bicycle spokes (e.g. https://www.youtube.com/watch?v=yZQw68diGcY).

Atigitigi – is a Lango traditional dance (e.g. https://www.youtube.com/watch?v=dgUH1iBJzZ8).

Ikoce – is a Lango Traditional dance (e.g. https://www.youtube.com/watch?v=4o3JhGyWzmw).

'**awal**' is calabash hollow drum   (in this video the men are using it as a dance instrument: https://www.youtube.com/watch?v=rI6d4SbWQ68).

'**tongo teke**' An Acholi traditional the elegant "forward-and-backward" dance move performed by women / girls (as illustrated in parts of this dance performance: https://www.youtube.com/watch?v=ir0TiHNyj-c).

'**piyo teke**' (An Acholi traditional elegant "side-to-side" dance move (as illustrated in parts of this dance performance: https://www.youtube.com/watch?v=ir0TiHNyj-c)

Muganda Drumming and dancing (e.g. at timeline 2:20 of this video: https://youtu.be/v47kNLyxlxY).

Banyangkole Drumming and dancing (e.g. https://youtu.be/ avCu7XqXeko).

Eritrean music dance tune (e.g. https://youtu.be/-AYuuJ57BsM).

Rwandan traditional Dance (e.g. https://youtu.be/RxDjiqPTIUg).

Kathakali Dance – This is one the Indian traditional dance that usually tells a story (e.g. https://youtu.be/_DNBgVAk9GE).

****

PART ONE

HUMBLE BEGINNINGS

Heavily pregnant, weak and weighed down, a young woman struggled with her every step as she walked through the wild fields all alone, all hope gone. She had been walking for days without seeing another human being. She was thirsty, hungry and had begun to feel increasing labour pains. With tears dropping down her eyes, she wondered: "How did it all come to this?! I had a good life in Otwe. I had a bright future, and it all got wiped away that dreadful afternoon on my way back from the market when the soldier attacked and raped me. Now I am all alone in this wilderness. I don't think I'll make it another day." She hopelessly thought to herself as she continued to walk-onwards.

 To avoid being re-captured again by armed men, she had been moving from place to place. An enormous stigma was attached to being raped, which caused so much shame, trauma, stress, anxiety and depression. She wanted to run away and hide. So far, she had travelled cross-country, ending up among a new tribal region which language she did not speak or understand. She was very far away from her people who could have helped and supported her.

Eventually when the labour pains overpowered her, she rested under the shade of a big tree, sweating and panting.   It so happened that an old woman from a nearby village was walking past the tree to forage for wild mushrooms. As she hunted for food, she heard a groaning sound punctuated with high pitched screams. On hearing a female's voice, she decided to check out what the noise was.

To her surprise, she found a young woman in agony, about to give birth. The old woman dropped everything and rushed to assist the pregnant lady. After what seemed like an eternity of pushing and heaving, her baby was born into the world. "It's a boy!" declared the old woman. With one final groan, the new mother exhaled a loud sigh and with her last breath said: "Gamme" which translates as 'take him.' To the old women (who could not speak or understand Acoli), it sounded as though the mother had muttered "Kamdenge!" so she assumed that this was the name the dying mother gave her new born son. Respectfully, she laid the new mother under the tree, covering her lifeless body with branches and carried out a short ritual asking the Gods to guard her, then quickly took the baby home.

Once she reached the village, she informed the elders of what had happened. They then arranged a simple, yet dignified burial for the young woman. Believing that the baby boy was a gift from the Gods to the old woman, they blessed her and the newborn child, giving instructions to take him and raise him as her own. Gladly, the old woman did as was told by the elders and cared for Kamdenge as her own.

In the village, was a young woman who had just lost her own baby at birth. The old woman made an arrangement with this bereaved mother, to breast-feed the little boy for her. There were several other mothers in the area who also had their babies around the same time that Kamdenge was born. So Kamdenge, the orphaned boy grew up being loved and cared for by a group of women, and made great friends with other children in the community.

There were four particular boys, who were his closest and best friends. Each of them had special nicknames based on the unique features or characteristic they had: Awange-acel (one-eyed), Akome-ikoyo (one who is always freezing cold), Ayie-lyet (always-hungry) and Abade-bor (long-arm). They would all play together, ate in one another's house, and had sleepovers. Their parents were very happy to see them getting on so well, loyally forming lasting friendships.

Kamdenge and his friends were hard working; willingly helping their families in the fields and at home. When the day's work was done, they knew how to enjoy their free time. Near the village, was a beautiful freshwater river where they bathed, did their laundry and drew water. Carefree, they spent many an hour playing and joyfully splashing around in the clear, refreshing river.

Just when Kamdenge was feeling very settled and grounded, his fortune changed. The old woman who was by his mother's side and helped him come into the world, passed away, leaving him homeless and empty handed. The families of Kamdenge's friends did their best to support him where they could, but having very little themselves, there wasn't much they could offer him. Thankfully, the bond between Kamdenge and his friends was so strong, and this is what kept him going, especially during times when life was very difficult for him.

Having no fixed abode, Kamdenge was looked down upon by the rest of society, as were his friends and their families because they were also poor. Despite living in poverty, they were happy for Kamdenge to take turns staying in their humble homes and offered him food and shelter, sharing the only riches they had: kindness and generosity. Transcending his trials, Kamdenge was resilient and grew up to be a very talented, handsome young man; full of grace, wisdom and knowledge. Together with his friends, who had their own unique characteristics, they always stood by each other.

****

Kamdenge and his friends lived in a remote village on the outskirts of a kingdom that had a very arrogant King. It was so far away that they were the very last people to hear about a proclamation issued by their King concerning the marriage of his beautiful daughter.

This most beautiful Princess was an only child. As he had no son and heir, the arrogant King decreed that whoever married his daughter would become joint heir, with his daughter, to his throne, and be given the title of 'His Royal Highness, the Prince.' There was no bride price to be paid for the dowry - any young man or bachelor was eligible, regardless of their financial status or background!

Instead of a dowry, the arrogant King set only three tests and the first suitor to pass all the tests would become the proud husband of his beautiful Princess. However, failing any of those tests came with a terrible price: it would cost the brave contender his life... The arrogant King did not want any failed suitor to reveal the three tests to any other men in the kingdom, who wanted the chance to obtain the hand of his precious daughter.

****

By the time Kamdenge heard this proclamation, so many young men had already gone to the palace, failed the tests and had lost their lives; the whole land was in great mourning. However, this did not deter Kamdenge, who thought that he stood a good chance of being successful in passing the tests. He decided to enroll for the contest, convinced he had nothing to lose and consulted with his four best friends, who also wished to challenge their arrogant King by accompanying him to the palace, even only for a chance to see what life looked like there, and also to taste the royal food!

To look the part, the five young men borrowed suitable attire from various people in the village who were better off than they were. They went to the river and meticulously washed themselves until they were squeaky-clean. There at the riverside, some young ladies scrubbed their calabashes with sand. They scrubbed until only the finest grains of sand remained. The fine grains of sand was then given to Kamdenge and his friends. Taking the fine grains between their index finger and thumb, the young men applied the tiny particles of sand to their teeth and began to gently rub. After a good rubbing, they rinsed off the sand using clean water, and then used softly crushed charcoal to polish their teeth until they sparkled and gleamed.

The five young men then went about making shampoo to wash their hair. They plucked some fresh tender branches of opobo (pobo) reeds from the banks of the river. Peeling off the outer bark to harvest the tender inner lining (phloem) from the core inner spine (Heartwood, the central supporting pillar of the tree branch), they crushed it to make it soft, and mixed it with water to create a shampoo out of the slippery sap. They rubbed some shea-nut-oil into their hair, and then they groomed it until not a single hair was standing out of place.

Once their ablutions were completed, the friends got dressed in their finery. The outfits they had borrowed fitted them so well; it was as if they had been tailor-made for them individually. With well-polished, shiny shoes completing the look, their appearance was transformed beyond recognition and made an overnight sensation within their village! Not a single male in the entire village, came close to matching Kamdenge and his friends 'appearance of status and attractiveness. All who saw them, were in total awe and full of admiration of these handsome fellows.

The village elders all came together to bless Kamdenge and his friends, and to see them off on their quest. They prayed with them and gave them a 'saliva blessing', a custom where an elder would sparingly spit his saliva in the recipient's palm to symbolise the blessing, prayers of well wishes and mercy for the journey.

Their families and friends gathered along the roadside to see them off and say their farewells. Respected old men and women blessed them, imparting words of wisdom, whilst the excited girls and boys who had congregated were whispering, giggling and point-ing at the totally transformed eligible young men! As the five of them walked past, the well-wishers chanted a song declaring how majestic they looked:

When the five

Walked the street

Even the grass

By the roadside

Seemed to bow

Down in homage

And so Kamdenge and his friends departed from their village, full of hope that they would be victorious in their mission.

****

PART TWO: A JOURNEY TO THE PALACE

As they embarked on their journey towards the palace, they met many characters upon their travels. First along the way they came across some Iwalu (crested crane) and Amuka (rhinoceros) from Lango. There was an air of sorrow from the passing travellers, who were in mourning. They were going to a funeral of one of their sons and son-in-law, who had lost their lives having failed the arrogant King's test.

The lead Iwalu asked Kamdenge where they were going, and he boldly told them:

"I am going to the palace to marry the King's daughter."

On hearing that the young men intended on going on the same mission that cost their own son his life, their grief deepened. They did not feel it wise for the young men to proceed. They were sad for Kamdenge for they felt that, if his parents were still alive, they would have advised against continuing on this ill-fated mission. They exclaimed:

"Oh! If your mother was here!"

Oh! If your father was here!"

"This would not happen. Now you are going to die!"

The Iwalu and Amuka started to sing a dirge in Lango:

Kamdenge! Kamdenge! Kamdenge, tin ito!

Kamdenge-denge-denge! Kamdenge, tin ito!

Kamdenge! Kamdenge! Kamdenge, tin ito!

Ai-doi! Atin kic, Kamdenge! tin ito!

Awobi a mwol, omini nyo amini moro pe, Kamdenge! tin ito oko!

Kamdenge! Kamdenge! Kamdenge, Surely you'll perish today!

Kamdenge-denge-denge! Kamdenge, You'll perish tonight!

Kamdenge! Kamdenge! Kamdenge, Surely you'll perish today!

Oh my dear orphan boy Kamdenge! You'll perish tonight!

Oh sweet man with no brother or sister, Kamdenge!

Surely you will perish tonight!

The Iwalu sang and danced to a Atigitigi dance rhythm, while the Amuka clouded the air with the dust their strong feet had unearthed, as they enthusiastically engaged in the 'ikoce 'dance rhythm. Kamdenge and his friends could not resist the inviting throbbing of the drums and joined in the dancing.

Kamdenge jumped high to the Atigitigi rhythm and his friends grooved to the Ikoce tempo. They were enjoying themselves so much, but the young men began to realise that time was against them and left the dance arena, and continued on their journey.

Further along the way, they met a flock of sacred Ibis birds all dressed in traditional Egyptian and Eritrean attire. One of the birds, the leader, enquired where Kamdenge and his friends were going.

"I am going to the palace to marry the King's daughter," said Kamdenge with an assertively proud gesture.

The birds, who knew how many suitors had already been killed at the palace, began crying and started singing an Eritrean dirge, that had the exact same sentiment as the Lango lamentation:

**Kamdenge! Kamdenge! Kamdenge! Brigts
lomi mishet kitmewt ika!**

Kamdenge! Kamdenge! Kamdenge! Lomi leyti ktmewt ika!

**Kamdenge! Kamdenge! Kamdenge! Niska brigits
lomi misht ktmewt ika!**

mskin zkeberka weledi albo Kamdenge! Lomi leyti kitmewt ika!

**mskin tsbuq sebay hawi albo wy hafti albo, Kamdenge! brigits
lomi leyti ktmewt ika.**

The lament was accompanied by traditional Eritrean tunes and dance styles. Kamdenge and his friends, not being put off by the concern for their lives, just enjoyed themselves by dancing along to the singing. When they realised that time was against them, they excused themselves and continued onwards on their journey.

After a little while they met the Baganda and Banyangkole 'peacocks, 'all dressed in Kigandan and Banyangkole traditional costumes. Like the previous groups they met, the leader asked Kamdenge where they were going.

"I am going to the palace to marry the princess!" he answered assertively with a gesture of assured confidence.

These peacocks too, began to mourn Kamdenge and his friends; they sang the dirge song in Luganda and then in Runyakore, with the exact same meaning as the lamentations before:

Luganda:

**Kamdenge!Kamdenge!
Kamdenge!**

**Daala ogenda nkusaanawo
olwaleero!**

Kamdenge!denge!

26

denge!Kamdenge
ogenda nkusaanawo olwaleero!

Maziima Mulekwa wange
owombulenzi!ogenda
nkusaanawo olwaleero!

Daala omushajja omwagalwa
atayina mugandawe!

Kamdenge ogenda nkusaanawo
olwaleero!

Runyakore:

Kamdenge!Kamdenge!
Kamdenge!

Amaziima nozakuch-
wechwelera ekikiiro!

Kamdenge!denge!
denge!Kamdenge!

nozakuchwechwelera ekikiiro!

Kamdenge!Kamdenge!
Kamdenge!nozakuch-
wechwelera ekikiiro!

Ayi enfuuzi yangye!nozaku-
chwechwelera ekikiiro!

Ayi Omushiijja mulungi,a-
taine mwinenyina!

Kamdenge nozakuch-
wechwelera ekikiiro!

Caught up in the moment, Kamdenge and his friends danced to the Muganda and Banyangkole drum rhythm tunes that were being played by the peacocks and became intoxicated by the visceral vibrations. Suddenly aware that much time had passed, they made a polite exit and hurried towards their destination.

Next, they met the Rwandan flamingos, all dressed in Kinyarwanda costumes. The lead flamingo asked them where they were going and Kamdenge answered in his unusually pompous manner,

"I am going to the palace to marry the Princess".

Straight away the flamingos started to lament in Kinyarwanda, singing the very same dirge in Kamdenge's name:

Kamudenge! Kamdenge! Irijoro urabura byanze bikunze!

Kamudenge! Denge-denge!
Kamudenge! Irijoro urabura!

ignoring all warnings of the danger that lay ahead if they continued, the young men eagerly joined in the singing and the beautiful Rwandan dance. After several hours had elapsed, they began to realise that time was against them and speedily went on their way towards the palace.

A little later, they met a group of Elephants from India, all dressed in colourful Indian costumes. The lead elephant asked Kamdenge where they were going dressed so elegantly. Kamdenge simply told them,

"I am going to the palace to marry the princess!"

Just like that, these elephants tried to discourage them from going on such a foolish mission that would be the end of their lives...

But by now, Kamdenge was more and more determined to reach the palace. He did not take heed to the warnings given by the distressed travellers that by proceeding, he and his friends would most likely lose their lives! His heart and mind was set on marrying the Princess and transforming his life from pauper to Prince. Blinded by his end goal, it did not even occur to him that he could also be risking the lives of his friends and they were in danger too. His improvidence and lack of concern for the perils he was heading towards and leading his friends to, deeply saddened the elephants, who ruefully lamented by singing the same dirge. Instantly the air was filled with a beautiful, yet mournful song. Everyone around started dancing to a Kathakali dance rhythm:

Kamdenge! Kamdenge! Kamdenge, Surely you'll perish today!

Kamdenge-denge-denge! Kamdenge, You'll perish tonight!

Kamdenge! Kamdenge! Kamdenge, Surely you'll perish today!

Oh my dear orphan boy Kamdenge! You'll perish tonight!

Oh sweet man with no brother or sister, Kamdenge!

Surely you will perish tonight!

Even though the Kathakali music and the dance told of a sad story, Kamdenge did not pay attention to the message in the beat. In complete ignorance, he and his friends joyfully danced to the rhythms of the drumbeat. Then all of a sudden, like someone waking from a deep sleep, Kamdenge remembered their journey ahead. He realised what his main mission was and he hurried his friends to move on with his quest for the Princess' hand.

When they were nearing the palace, they met Til (antelopes) and Dolo (Colobus monkeys) from the Acholi land. Agitatedly, they were pacing up and down and were speaking with everyone they saw going towards the palace. Earlier on that day, they had met a group of people who were returning from the burial of one or more of their loved ones, whom the arrogant King had put to death, after failing the tests he had set as a 'dowry 'for his daughter.

Both the Til and 'Dolo, having lost their own sons and sons-in-law, stood like gate keepers to prevent any more young men from entering the palace in vain. As Kamdenge lead his friends towards the gates of doom, the Dolo asked him:

"Where are you going?"

With a very cheerful manner, Kamdenge confidently replied: "I'm going to the palace to marry the Princess!"

For Dolo, this foolish answer triggered very painful memories of numerous young men having already lost their lives. Each of them, one after another, had gone to the palace to ask for the hand of the daughter of their arrogant King. None left the palace alive. The whole kingdom, apart from Kamdenge and his friends, were in mourning. His heart set on marrying the Princess, no one was going to stop him - not after coming this far!

However much the Til and the Dolo tried to convince Kamdenge and his friends not to enter the palace, their efforts were in vain. Kamdenge was determined to reach the palace. As a result, the Til and his company, washed their hands of them and instead, sang a dirge song in lamentation of the foolish men. They sang some painful traditional Acholi funeral songs in Kamdenge's name that had identical meaning to the previous dirges:

> **Kamdenge! Kamdenge!**
> **Kamdenge, tin ibito ba!**
>
> **Kamdenge-denge-denge!**
> **Kamdenge , tin ibito!**
>
> **Kamdenge! Kamdenge!**
> **Kamdenge, tin ibito ba!**

Ai latin kic, Kamdenge!
tin ibito!

Awobi ma mwol, omeru
nyo lameru mo pe,
Kamdenge! tin ibito ba!

The drummers beat their drums with renewed vigour, and the dancers careened to the rhythm of the sorrowful funeral song, as if pre-mourning these ignorant 'Ojuk-kwe' young men. More and more people congregated, joining in the singing and dancing to the 'Otole' tune rhythm. After a little while, they turned to the 'Acut 'rhythm, which was usually an all-female prayer dance, but by this time, everyone started to participate in an entreaty for the lives of Kamdenge and his friends.

Within a short time, the sound of the drumming and music had drawn a very large audience. Some younger men, who had some feathers on their heads, started to blow their flutes, attracting several elegant ladies to engage in the 'Dingi – Dingi 'rhythm, which is an all-female choreographed dance. The drummers were beating their drums with such energy; drawing in more young men who joined in with their 'awal 'and ciliki'. With that, they stylishly beat on their 'awal 'so fervently, exuding very exciting, traditional music.

They created a semi-circle opposite a line of smart, colourfully dressed, elegant young women who were dancing with vigour. Working their waists and necks so gracefully, you would be forgiven for thinking that they had no bones in their lithe bodies.

The drummers then changed the beat to that of the 'Larakaraka '(pronounced, 'la-ra-ka-ra-ka') rhythm and dance. This is a courtship dance where each girl takes it in turn to show off her moves and talent, by vigorously gyrating, jiggling and thrusting her waist.

A young woman approached Kamdenge and began to elegantly

perform the 'tongo teke' and 'piyo teke' dances before him. Handed traditional instruments, he lifted up an 'awal' in one hand, and with the other, beat it to the rhythm. Kamdenge then began dancing around the young lady, like the way a cock courts a hen.

Kamdenge's stylish dance moves really spurred on the girl, who in turn showed off her best dance moves to him. As they wildly danced, Kamdenge whispered something in her ear, and then crowned her with his awal. This symbolic gesture delighted the girl who smiled and gave an amazing performance to him. Before handing the musical instruments back to the owner, Kamdenge continued to dance with the girl in front of the crowds that had started to gather.

At the palace gate there were a number of tourists waiting for permission to enter and tour the royal grounds. When they saw what was happening, they were consumed with the Acholi cultural beat. Pairing up with their partners, they indulged in their Western style ballroom dances and waltzing. Some even started break-dancing, while others strutted around in a Tango dance style. The Masai men at the gate jumped up and down high into the sky, while singing the Kamdenge dirge in Swahili:

> **Kamdenge! Kamdenge! Kamdenge! Hakika
> utaangamia usiku huu!**
>
> **Kamdenge! denge-denge! Kamdenge!
> Utaangamia usiku huu!**
>
> **Kamdenge! Kamdenge! Kamdenge! Hakika
> utaangamia usiku huu!**
>
> **Aah! mpendwa wangu kijana yatima Kamdenge!
> Utaangamia usiku huu!**
>
> **Aah! mwanaume mzuri usiye na kaka wala dada,**
>
> **Kamdenge! Hakika utaangamia usiku huu!**

Enraptured in the revelry, all these different dance styles left Kamdenge and his friends very exuberant; they completely forgot the reason why they had made the journey to the palace. With the fervour of the dancing and drumming, they had shaken off all nerves and anxieties. Full of high-spirited boldness and excitement, they confidently entered the palace gate like celebrities.

IN THE PALACE

Once inside the palace compound, the first thing they noticed were several magnificent buildings. The gardens and footpaths were immaculate. There were beautiful arrays of colourful flowers, perfectly manicured lawns, well-kept shrub fences and plentiful strategically placed trees. Uniformed soldiers guarded the palace, some people were working and some walking around the compound. There was a solemn atmosphere; there were no children playing, there was no singing, laughter or chatter. Just silence.

Tired from their journey and from all the dancing they did along the way, Kamdenge and his friends arrived very late in the evening. Upon their arrival, they were given a very warm royal welcome that exceeded their expectations. The most delicious meal they had ever tasted in their lives was served to them as guests to the palace.

Following the feast, they were each shown to their luxurious en-suite rooms where they would spend the night to rest. Knowing that this could be their last night alive, they decided to thoroughly enjoy all the pleasures and comforts being offered them.

They were so thrilled to hear that they would be meeting the King the following morning after a mouth-watering royal breakfast. At least that would give them one more helping of a royal meal before anything could happen to them.

A MATTER OF LIFE OR DEATH

DAY ONE: THE FIRST TEST

The following morning, soon after the breakfast feast, Kamdenge and his friends were summoned before the arrogant King, who briefed them about the tests to be undertaken to win the hand of the Princess. He had decided that since his friends had accompanied Kamdenge this far, they should accompany him to the very end; enduring all the challenges with him. Only one test would be given each day and the King would be given the result after breakfast the next morning.

Kamdenge was informed that his first test was to do with food. This delighted the party of five greatly, knowing that they now had the rare opportunity to savour royal cuisines and dine like a King; something that had been completely out of their reach. With their minds all caught up in the privileges they were enjoying, the five young men did not think twice about accepting the challenge. So when they were invited into a dining room for their first test, they were full of excitement for what lay ahead.

Completely consumed with uncontrollable ecstasy, they entered the room where they were to take their first test. The room was exquisitely decorated and in the middle, was the biggest banqueting table they had ever seen; laden with deliciously mouth-watering food. The young men could not believe their eyes - it was more than all the food they had ever eaten in their lives!

A big fattened bull had been slaughtered, and different cuts of meat from the animal were prepared and cooked in different styles for Kamdenge and his friends. There were abundant fruits, bread, cakes and desserts that they had never seen before in their lives. Plates were piled high with wild black grapes, bunches of sweet bananas (Abolo Amemo), and juicy oversized oranges. To wash down the food, there were giant jugs of freshly pressed Tugu juice (from the Deli palm or Borassus palm), jugs of cool spring water along with intricately carved, designer-made calabashes carefully arranged on the table: it was a dream come true for these men who knew only too well what hunger felt like.

The challenge was set: in order to pass the first test they had to eat and clear the food on the table by midnight. Not a single morsel or crumb was to be left. Should they fail to complete eating up all the food that night, they would have failed the test and would be put to death.

Disregarding the possibility of failing the test, Kamdenge and his friends did not waste even a second to think things through. Dashing over to tuck in to the mountainous feast, they eagerly began to munch their way through the gourmet food. They ate and ate until Kamdenge and three of them could eat no more, but there was still plenty of food on the table. Even though they were full, they exchanged jokes about how they had always yearned to taste royal cuisines. Gradually, the bites they took got smaller and smaller until it became too much - four of them struggled to digest even the tiniest of crumbs! Full to the brim, they slumped their heads against the table, to doze off having exhausted themselves by over-eating.

It had not occurred to them that their other friend, Ayie-lyet (Always-hungry), was still going strong and carried on eating. He continued to munch his way through the food, eating bit by bit. By night fall the other four had just fallen into a deep sleep, leaving Ayie-lyet still devouring what they could not eat.

The soldiers on shift, took it in turns to keep watch to make sure that there was no cheating. There was always three men on duty at a time, with the one having been there the longest being relieved by the next to report. It was vital that they monitored Kamdenge and his friends to ensure that no food was wasted, or thrown away. They had to check that every last morsel was eaten up, as the King had instructed that the test was to be carried out with accuracy, and transparency.

Ayie-lyet continued to eat and eat; not in the slightest bit concerned that all his friends had now fallen asleep! By the time the clock struck midnight, he had finished eating and was just swallowing the last mouthful of food on the table. This surprised the soldiers on guard watching - they could not believe what they had just witnessed: these five young men had cleared every single crumb from the table! The stunned soldiers just stood with their mouths agape and their eyes wide open in sheer disbelief at the astonishing feat.

The following day after breakfast, the King was informed that Kamdenge and his friends had passed his first test very successfully. Unconvinced, he accused his guards of collaborating with the suitor in rigging the result, and had them all thrown in a dark room, where they were all put to death. He then selected another three of his most trusted soldiers to closely monitor the second test. The King sternly commanded that they constantly kept strict guard over the contestant's party during the second test, with the upmost diligence. It was imperative that they did not take their eyes off Kamdenge and his friends. The test would start that evening, after dinner.

****

DAY TWO: THE SECOND TEST

Enjoying their freedom after successfully passing the royal-feast test, Kamdenge and his comrades were all ready for his second challenge. They were especially thankful and grateful to Ayie-lyet, who had enabled them to pass their first test and saved their lives. Without him, they would have been killed by now.

The details of the next trial were given and they were informed that they would all spend the night together in one room. Not suspecting anything, to them, this would only give them a chance to discuss and share their experiences of royal-life so far. Having been spared because of Ayie-lyet and his ability to eat so much, this blinded them from anticipating what danger lay ahead: they would be spending the night in a torture chamber!

That evening, Kamdenge and his four friends were relocated to a very small room - with no ventilators! This room was quite warm inside to start with, but it gradually became hotter and hotter. Throughout the night, the temperature kept increasing until it had soared past 40 degrees centigrade. There was no water inside; the door and windows were fully locked from the outside so there was absolutely no way the friends could escape. They were in so much discomfort: drenched in sweat, their throats dried, and it felt as if they were suffocating. Regardless of how hard they knocked on the door or shouted for help, no one came to their rescue, yet they could hear the guards talking outside. The guards had no intention of coming to their rescue, they simply ignored them - as if they had heard nothing!

Kamdenge and his friends started to realise that they would not survive the night and come out of the room alive… But just when it seemed as if they were doomed to perish in the stifling cell and all hope was lost, Kamdenge and three of his friends suddenly felt an ooze of a cool breeze, which felt like a cold wind sweeping across the room. In an instant, the temperature of the roasting room was regulated drastically.

Hyped up by the miraculous change of circumstance, they wondered how on earth this had happened. Akome-ikoyo (one who is always freezing cold) then revealed his unzipped jacket. The icy-cold wind had flowed from him and wafted through the room, adjusting the intolerable temperature! And with that, the five men spent the entire night in a very comfortable room, reminiscing on what had happened to them so far.

The friends became hopeful and began making plans for what they would do when Kamdenge became a Prince. Long conversations went on throughout the night, so much so that they did not sleep a wink and by the time they noticed the door was being opened, it was morning. They had successfully passed the second test and there was now, just one more task left to go! Surprised to find Kamdenge and his friends alive, the soldiers on guard released them, and instructed them to go and freshen up for breakfast.

On discovering that the second test had been passed, the arrogant King was infuriated and demanded that Kamdenge and his companions were brought before him immediately. He had them examined thoroughly, but no sign of burns or dehydration were found on any of them, which enraged the King even more. Baffled, he could not understand how Kamdenge and his friends had spent the entire night in the furnace room, and had withstood such extreme heat. Indeed, the room had been as hot as a baker's oven, or a potter's kiln.

In his fury, the maddened King ordered all the soldiers who had kept guard that night, to be thrown inside the room where the suitor had spent the night with his friends. He then commanded that the door and windows be locked from the outside. To prevent the soldiers from escaping, the keys were handed to the Royal Treasury for safe keeping. The cruel King had no intention of releasing the guards, whom he suspected of conspiring with the suitor to cheat and defraud the test. The poor soldiers perished in the furnace room in punishment.

DAY THREE

Perplexed by what had happened in his palace, the King paced up and down with both his hands tightly crossed behind his back with a distant look upon his face. For a little while the King fixed his gaze far away, trying to make sense of the situation, and to clear his foggy mind. He fidgeted with his fingers, and his beady eyes darted around as if looking for answers where none could be found. His tight lips were pursed as he ground his clenched teeth in rage.

Stopping suddenly, he tossed his head upwards and sideways, like a ploughing ox does when it is angry from being driven so hard. His bodyguards who were following him at a reasonable distance, quickly rushed to his side to see if there was anything they could do. Aware of their presence, the King dramatically turned to face them and commanded, "Go! Gong the bell and summon the entire troop of officers here immediately!" The bell was gonged to summon the officers; whilst a rap song was being chanted:

Right away

The guard dashed

The bell gonged - loudly

The officers all came - running

To pay respect to - their king

Each officer knew his role at the palace and when the King uttered stern orders, they each knew what to do immediately. In a chanting rap song, the King's command was given:

"Quick!

Prepare for the Royal,
Marriage feast.

Right away!

Give the suitor and his comrades

The best royal - marriage attire

For the wedding -
ceremony tonight!

Send words to - the entire
kingdom,

Invite everybody to -
attend without fail!

I will inform - the queen

And - the Princess."

With that, the officers suddenly vanished like a thick cloud disappearing after a strong stormy wind.

****

THE THIRD AND FINAL TEST:

Kamdenge and his friends were all dressed up in their best royal marriage attires, as the King had ordered. They waited inside the palace private wing. Although they had been offered 'Lira-Lira' (a distilled alcoholic drink); they decided against drinking least it clouded their judgment for the final test. Instead, they had opted for a refreshing tamarind juice. They enjoyed the drink, but anticipated what the final test would be.

In the middle of the palace grounds there was a deep, spring - water well, where on important occasions, guests of the Royal Family were entertained. The water source had a secure lockable cover on top, which was adorned with an array of dazzling and colourful potted flowers.

All the invited guests of the kingdom had arrived. They had come from far and wide and had assembled in the palace ground to witness this extraordinary event. The venue was brimming with so many guests: *'Langwidi matar rabo ki-cen!'*

At the appointed time, the King and his Queen ceremoniously emerged, proudly holding the hand of their daughter, the Princess between them. Dressed in an array of the most expensive costumes, the guests marvelled at the luxury never seen in the entire kingdom before.

The King sat on his throne, facing a sea of eyes that were fixed intently upon him. He then commanded that Kamdenge and his friends be brought before him for their third and final test.

There was a sharp intake of breath from the astonished onlookers as Kamdenge majestically emerged with his four best friends before the King. Such a grand appearance of the Royal suitor rendered all who saw him speechless. There was a stillness in the air as the subjects of the land gazed at Kamdenge in awe and wonderment. The Queen and Princess were agape when they set eyes on him for the first time, as he looked so dashingly handsome and majestic in his wedding attire. Standing before them, Kamdenge bowed gracefully in homage and then slowly lifted his head and laid his eyes upon the Princess.

This disarmed the King, who was full of discomfort at the hushed silence that filled the courtyard. To assert his authority, he cleared his throat to demand the attention of the expectant crowds. Breaking out into a smile, dimples as deep as a well appeared on both his cheeks. His sharp eyes twinkled and glinted - an expression that had never before been seen by his subjects, who stood shoulder to shoulder, shocked by his uncharacteristic demeanour.

Turning to the Princess, the King smiled at his beloved daughter. He then looked at the Queen and gave a nod of approval and gave a small wink. His eyes then met those of the crowds', who waited with great anticipation. Regally, he turned towards his wife and gave her a second nod of approval then gesticulated to indicate that it was now time to move into action.

****

The Queen majestically rose from her throne and elegantly glided through the crowds, towards the lake in the palace compound. As she did this, a chanting rap song narrated her actions:

The Queen then rose
up, majestically

Holding a beautiful golden
ring between her thumb

and the index fingure

Her little finger sticking
out so proudly!

She fixed her eyes
upon Kamdenge

Then she walked
grandly straight to

The mouth of the deep
spring water

well, adorned with
sapphires & diamonds.

Surrounded by colourful
& beautiful

Potted flower arrangements

She raised her hand, still
holding the gold wedding ring,

Above and over the water well

And then she let go of the
gold wedding ring

Right into, and straight through
and down to the bottom

Of that very deep-deep
spring water well

****

Then, the Queen gracefully laid her hand on her chest and looked back at Kamdenge with motherly eyes. Her body swayed as she took stately steps back towards her throne and ceremoniously took her seat. Lovingly, she regarded her daughter and husband before allowing her maternal eyes to fall on Kamdenge.

After the resplendent display from the Queen, the King rose before the crowds. He beheld his wife and they exchanged knowing smiles. Proudly adoring his beautiful Princess, he took her hand and raised her from her throne to a chorus of cheerful applause from the excited crowd. The Royal Family stood before the entire kingdom, the King cleared his throat and addressed his assembled subjects:

"My beloved people, today we are all gathered here to witness the marriage of your Princess, my beautiful daughter, to this very handsome young man, Kamdenge."

As he said this, he offered an outstretched hand towards Kamdenge with a genuine smile, who bowed in respect, as did his comrades. This caused such a stir that even the Queen applauded the presentation of her future son-in-law. The audience roared with rounds of rapturous applause, the women raised their voices and made joyous 'kijira' sounds and the men responded by 'mwoco mwoc'. The cacophony could be heard for miles and miles beyond the palace.

Patiently, the King waited for his subjects to calm and quieten.

"However," interrupted the King with an authoritative beckoning of his hand. You could hear a pin drop at the sudden silence. The King continued. "But there is still one last test that the suitor must pass before the marriage ceremony can commence." Pausing in earnest and with his hand stretched out as a gesture of good will, he then went on to warmly address Kamdenge:

"Is that not so Mr Kamdenge, my future son-in-law, the Prince-to-be?"

A broad smile appeared on his face that left a twinkle in his eyes. Gracious glances were exchanged between the Royal family and the radiant Princess fixed her gaze upon her father, waiting for him to announce what the final test would be. The muted crowd held their breath and began to wonder what was happening; it looked as though there was a sign of tears in the King's eye!

Regaining composure, he coughed deeply to clear his throat from the salty tears that had momentarily left him choked. Aware of the multitude of eyes that stared blankly at him, Kamdenge stood, stately poised with firm reassurance, ready to accept the final test.

Finally, after what felt like an eternity to the Princess and the crowd, the King cleared his throat again and then addressed Kamdenge,

"Now, my beloved son–to-be, I want you to pay attention to me very carefully, and listen to everything that I am going to tell you."

The King then pointed to the spot where the Queen had earlier stood, by the mouth of the deep spring water well, surrounded with the beautiful potted-floral arrangements. Continuing, he explained the task:

"Down there, at the bottom of that deep spring water well, there is a gold wedding ring. You must retrieve the ring and put it on the Princess' finger. That would be the bridal price you need for the hand of my beautiful daughter."

With that, the King slowly sat back on his throne, as if in anticipation that something could go wrong and jeopardise the wedding. He now found himself in a dilemma: he already loved Kamdenge and did not wish to lose him; he was also aware of the conditions he had set regarding the tests. Not wanting to look weak, foolish or lose his power, he felt there was no way he could withdraw from his side of the bargain. Neither did he want Kamdenge to fail the test, as he had warmed to him being his son-in-law. Should Kamdenge lose, the King would lose his daughter as he would be the one responsible for the death of her future husband, who had come so close to winning her hand.

Shocked by the impossible challenge that Kamdenge faced, the Princess stood in stunned silence, just staring in disbelief at her despotic father. She opened her mouth and tried to say something, but no words came out. Deploringly, she looked at her mother with desperate eyes, as if to ask her to say something to the King, but this was only met with a sanguine smile. The Princess anxiously looked at Kamdenge, but when she encountered the stately tranquil demeanour on her fiancé's comforting face, she became calm and sat back down again, next to her father. Her mother followed suit and took her place on her throne.

The crowds were left speechless as Kamdenge silently bowed down in homage to the King. Their eyes followed every move he made, and they looked on with a mixture of admiration and pity. Kamdenge raised himself up slowly and, looking at his future wife, he smiled. His reassurance eased the anxiety that had gripped the Princess and all the guests.

Then, turning to his comrades, Kamdenge acknowledged the willingness in their eyes and he nodded with satisfaction. His friends returned the gesture and nodded back in acceptance. They were all going to undertake the final challenge. To the astonishment of the myriad of people looking on, Kamdenge and his four friends walked with dignified assertiveness up to the mouth of the well which led to the deep, spring water reservoir.

Without any equipment or special tools, they set about retrieving the ring from the deep water with their bare hands. Full of dismay, the guests watched with growing consternation as the five men knelt down at the edge of the deep-deep spring water well. The Royals were bemused by what they were witnessing; Kamdenge and two of his friends, Ayie-lyet (Always-hungry), and Akome-ikoyo (One who is always freezing cold), were instructed by Awange-acel (One-eyed), to step aside, leaving just Abade-bor (Long-arms) and Awange-acel (One-eyed) still on their knees.

These two men moved closer to the mouth of the deep-deep spring water well, up to the very spot where the Queen had dropped the precious ring. It was at this point that the crowd started to notice something different about the Royal Groom's friends. Apart from

Kamdenge, each of the four men accompanying him had unique physical features about them.

They noticed that Abade-bor, who was attempting to retrieve the gold wedding ring from the depths of the water, seemed to have an abnormally long expandable arm and only had one hand. It became apparent that it was with this long arm that he was trying to reach the bottom of the well. His comrade Awange-acel, who had only one eye, was doing all he could in directing Abade-bor accordingly, towards the spot where the band of gold lay.

It appeared as though Awange-acel' also had a unique feature about him: his one eye had an exceptional telescopic ability with which he could see the tiniest of things, even from a long distance. Remarkably, he was actually able to see the gold wedding ring at the bottom of the deep-deep spring water well. That way he was able to work well with Abade-bor. He was trying hard to direct the hand of his colleague to the exact spot where the wedding ring was. His ability to clearly see through the water had enabled him to locate exactly where the gold wedding ring had fallen. It had landed on a cushion of glittering sand at the bottom of the deep spring water well.

These two groom's men worked diligently together in a harmonising manner, and they soon recovered the gold wedding ring from depths of spring water well. Abade-bor promptly handed it to Kamdenge, who jubilantly raised it up to reveal the precious and magnificent wedding ring to the crowd. The crowd roared with excitement, applauding Kamdenge and his friends with a standing ovation. The women went wild with excitement making the 'kijira 'sounds: *'Aboka lam, twara ineno ki wangi'*

Without wasting a moment, Kamdenge proudly dried the wedding band, and walked with dignified strides to the Royal suite; the precious ring securely held between his right thumb and the middle finger, in front of him. He bowed down with his other hand behind his back like a waiter serving food or drink. As he did this, he lovingly fixed his eyes upon his Princess and respectfully addressed the King: 'Your Royal Highness!'

At this point the crowd started to quietly rise to their feet, quick to be the first one to jump in celebration at such a rare moment. Hearts pounding, each of them eagerly waited with their hands clasped together upon their chests, ready to explode in applause. As soon as the King had nodded in approval, Kamdenge triumphantly stood and beamed at his Princess.

Elegantly, the Princess ascended from her throne and stepped forward, and knelt down before Kamdenge. Reaching for her left hand, he proudly slipped the gold wedding ring on his bride's wedding finger, and tenderly kissed it. Brimming with elation, Kamdenge rose up, took his wife by the hand and chivalrously helped her to her feet. Standing before the jubilant crowd, he proudly showed off the beautiful band of gold on the Princess' finger - an affirmation of his royal entitlement. The once arrogant King, now his father-in-law, had kept his promise.

The palace became engulfed in the roaring applause and cheers from the people of the land, who went wild with excitement at this remarkable event. For the first time, it took the King many attempts to try to calm down his ecstatic subjects, who continued to rejoice in celebration. It was quite a while before the hubbub subsided in the palace and the King was able to proceed. No sooner had he managed to finish his proclamation to Kamdenge and his Princess,

"With my own authority, which is invested in me by divine power, I now pronounce you Husband and Wife!"

the crowd went into an unstoppable explosive celebratory frenzy, the like of which had never been seen or heard before in the entire history kingdom: 'Agana lam twara inn iwangi!'

The Royal Wedding party descended from the rostrum into the crowds, who parted the way for the historic ceremonious parade.

PART THREE

A NEW BEGINNING

The King, who had been renowned for his arrogant nature, had surprised everyone by keeping his word and swallowing his pride. He declared a week of feasting celebrations in the palace for which everybody was invited. As a gift to his Kingdom, he generously issued a week of public holidays across the land in honour and celebration of the Royal Wedding.

He made Kamdenge his second in command, honouring him with the title: 'His Royal Highness, Prince Kamdenge,' which afforded him many benefits, entitlements and freedoms. Kamdenge's four friends were awarded royal titles with high posts in the kingdom. Their lives were transformed and they were each given fully-furnished royal properties and land, together with wives and servants.

Over the wedding celebration weeks, the King spent more time with the newly crowned Prince Kamdenge, who told him about how they had managed to pass all the tests he had set for them. The King was the last person to realise that each one of Kamdenge's friends, had unique characteristics and special qualities about them.

During the feasting, the King noticed that one of the men seemed to have an enormous belly. It was at this point that the King learned that it was Ayie-lyet's ability to eat an enormous amount of food before feeling satisfied and full, that enabled them to successfully complete the first test.

Intrigued, the King again inquired as to why Akome-ikoyo wore a thick winter jacket all the time, even when the temperature was very hot. Kamdenge enlightened the King explaining that Akome-ikoyo was always frozen, so he constantly wore an extraordinarily heavy jacket not only to keep out the wintry cold, but to prevent the bitter chill from his body oozing out and blasting everybody around like a bad winter storm. In the second test when the chamber became very hot, Akome-ikoyo had unzipped his jacket releasing a cool breeze, which helped to regulate the temperature inside the room to a bearable state. Hearing this, the King was amazed by this extraordinary ability.

Likewise, the King was told about Abade-bor and how his long arm gave him the power to reach down to the bottom of the deep-deep spring water well and retrieve the gold wedding ring. Abade-bor had worked in collaboration with Awange-acel. Although Awange-acel only had one eye, this one eye was telescopic thus enabling him to see to the deepest depths of waters. He used his telescopic powers to locate the gold wedding ring from the bottom of the deep-deep spring water well and then directed the long-armed Abade-bor to retrieve the band of gold. Astonished by these incredible men and how they worked together to support their friend, the King felt humbled by this account and nodded in approval.

Wanting to get to know his new son-in-law, the King learned all about Kamdenge's life story: how he grew up an orphan with very little and how his friends always kept his spirits high, despite the challenges they all faced in life. The King listened intently about how Kamdenge had a humble beginning, how he hailed from nowhere, how he was a nobody without any known ancestry. Feeling protective over his son-in-law, the King saw that Kamdenge deserved to become a Prince, a Royal Highness with all his needs attended to, and to have a beautiful Princess for a wife!

****

CREDITS

I would like to thank, acknowledge, and credit the following people for their contributions to this book:

Rachel Regan *(Editor)*

Halima Brewer *(Editor)*

Tumaini *(Editor, Cover Design)*

Jimmy Amone *(Photographer)*

Jeff Slade *(Photographer)*

Daniel Kadokwac *(use of photograph)*

Lakica Festo-Magiri *(use of photograph)*

Sarah *(use of photograph)*

Martin Okwir *(use of photograph)*

Twonto Ronald Lameck *(photographer, use of photograph)*

Emmanuel Ocen *(use of photograph)*

Ogwang Gift Solomon *(use of photograph)*

Anonymous *(use of photograph)*

Festo Magiri *(translation)*

Eden Habtemicael *(Translation)*

Saidat Mirembe *(Translation)*

Ritah *(Translation)*

Caritas Umulisa *(Translation)*

ACKNOWLEDGEMENTS

First and foremost, I sincerely thank and appreciate the Lord God, for sustaining me and my passion for storytelling & writing, which he has preserved through all the trials I persevered through. It is only through his grace that I have come this far. I give him glory, honour and my deepest appreciation.

I also extend my thanks and gratitude to the following individuals, who, without their contributions and support, this book would not have been written:

In particular, I'd like to give special thanks to my daughters, and grandson, who have always stood by me and supported me in various ways. They put up with me, served me endless cups of teas and brought me food when I was writing this story. They were my first editors, whom I called upon from time to time when I was stuck for the right words, or phrase. A special thanks to Rachel Regan who brough in her passion and skills, in editing the Kamdege story.

My grandchildren, and their next generations, BK.LUWO and ATAT were the backbone, and have deepened my desire for storytelling, which led me to writing the story of Kamdenge. Mr. Richard Pinner was my Storytelling Lecturer at the University of Derby. I wrote and presented the Kamdenge story in one of his classes and I gained inspiration from this. Dr. Sam Kasule's advice on tradition and culture, were vital in guiding me in writing this story. He read my drafts, and offered invaluable and constructive feedback. Upon graduating, I encouraged the refugee women from BK.LUWO to write about their life stories as a form of therapy, as well as to preserve their valuable rich heritages, and to pass them down to the generations of children being born and raised up in the diaspora.

My daughters have continued this preservation and started the African Dance workshops for the community to promote health and wellbeing. They took their African Dance workshops to various schools and enriched the community by sharing our cultural heritage. They planned to have the Kamdenge story enacted as a theatrical musical dance performance, with the aim to reach the wider community, the asylum seekers, and those in detention. I approached Isabel Knowland and Arne Richards (Joint Artistic Directors, Oxford Concert Party). Together, with the support of Anthony Lloyd of the Oxford Concert Project, Pat Winslow (a renounced Storyteller, and artist), they then took on the Kamdenge tale to Kirtlington Primary School, where I told my story: the children were "entranced" . The Headmistress and the staff of the school then encouraged the pupils to perform the Kamdenge story as a play. Joy Mead had worked with me on this story to find a publisher. My daughter decided to enter this Kamdenge story for the Kindle Storyteller Award. Then the community of Lango Association UK had opened a virtual traditional storytelling platform, "Wii Otem", where those in the diaspora are encouraged to engage in the old tradition of oral storytelling. When I told the Kamdenge Story, the feedback was very encouraging. This rekindled my passion for this tale, which I heard at school when I was a child. The story has stayed with me ever since.

I am not able to accord my grandchildren the privilege of listening to traditional oral storytelling round the fireplace, neither would they be able to hear our rich traditional, and educational storytelling in their schools, here in the diaspora. My grandchildren, Malaikah, Tyrhys, and all my loved ones born and growing up in the diaspora, have all motivated and inspired me to start writing stories in the first place, most of all the Kamdenge story. I now dedicate the Kamdenge story to them.

****

Made in United States
Troutdale, OR
04/04/2024

18957100R00037